The Sharing Lion

Efrat Haddi

Illustrations - Abira Das

The Sharing Lion

Written by Efrat Haddi
Illustrations by Abira Das

Copyright c 2014 by Efrat Haddi

First edition – 08/2014

Leo, a lion cub, lived with his family in the jungle of Africa.

He had two best friends, Rose and Crown. Rose, a lioness, was about the same age as he was and Crown was a younger lion cub.

The three lions loved to play together. One morning they pursued a flock of butterflies in the field.

"Leo and Rose," yelled Crown suddenly. "Look, I found a cave."

The three friends carefully approached the cave entrance. It was very dark and it was difficult to see inside.

"It looks like a very large cave," said Leo. "I wonder what's inside it." "We shouldn't go inside the cave," said Crown. "There might be a large animal in there and it might attack us. Let's get out of here. I'm afraid." "We really shouldn't enter the cave," said Rose. "It is a big, dark cave. What will happen if we will lose our way and can't get out?"

"I have to see what's inside the cave," said Leo. "I'm not afraid." Leo did feel a little scared but he didn't want to let his friends know.

"Are you sure you want to enter?" asked Rose. "What if something bad happens to us?"

"Nothing bad will happen to us," said Leo, "We will be careful and watch over one another."

"Ok," said Rose. "I'll go behind you," said Crown, and all three went into the cave.

The three friends walked slowly and carefully.

The cave was very large and they could hear the sound of water dripping down from the ceiling. They saw that the water had created a small pond on the floor.

They noticed that there was an opening on the cave's ceiling, which let a few rays of sunlight into the cave and lit it up with a dim light.

A flock of bats were hanging from the cave's ceiling and when they saw the three lions they flew out quickly through the opening.

"Ugh, I hate bats," said Crown.

"Look, I see something shimmering at the edge of the cave," whispered Rose.

Leo and Crown looked where she was pointing .At the far wall of the cave, they saw a small shelf made of stone. On top of the shelf was something sparkling in red color.

"You're right," said Leo. "Let's go see what it is."

As they approached the far wall of the cave, they saw a big diamond-shaped red gemstone.

The rays of sun that were coming through the ceiling of the cave shed light on the stone and made it sparkle.

"Wow, what a beautiful gem," said Rose as she approached it.

"I've never seen such a beautiful gem," said Crown as he watched it sparkle.

"I told you that we should go into the cave," said Leo. "This is the most beautiful gem I've ever seen and I'll take it."

"But I also want the gem," said Rose.

"I want it too," said Crown.

"What do you mean?" said Leo, "I took you into the cave, so therefore the gem should be mine."

"I saw the sparkling gem first," said Rose. "Therefore the gem should be mine."

"That's not fair," said Crown. "I discovered this cave and therefore the gem should be mine."

They argued and argued and were unable to reach a decision about who will get to keep the sparkling gem.

"Let's take the gem to Brave, my father," said Leo, after the three friends were tired of arguing. "He is the leader of the pack. We will tell him what happened and he will decide who should get to keep the gem."

"Agreed," said Crown and Rose.

Leo tried to take the gem but the gem didn't move. He tried to move it with his hands and mouth but nothing happened.

"Let me try," said Rose but she also was unable to move the gem. Crown also tried to move the gem without success.

"Very strange," said Leo," We can't take it. Let's go talk to my father and then we will come back here."

All three lions walked out of the cave and went looking for Brave.

They found Brave sitting under his favorite giant tree watching the valley below.

"Hello there," said Brave when he saw the three young lions running towards him.

"Hi Dad," said Leo. "We need your help. Today while we were playing, Crown found a large cave. I persuaded my friends to go in and see what was inside. When we were inside, Rose saw a beautiful shiny red gem. We all want the gem and can't decide who should get it."

"And why don't all of you share the gem?" asked Brave.

"It is impossible to share this beautiful gem," said Leo. "If we break it, all its beauty will disappear and no one will be able to play with it."

"You don't need to break the gem," said Brave. "You are all best friends right?"

"Yes," they all replied. "We are very good friends and love to play together."

"Good friends should know how to share," said Brave. "Do you know why?"

"Why?" they asked.

"When good friends share," said Brave. "All of them can enjoy more. In order to share, each one of you must give up a little so that the others can enjoy too. This is what good friends do. For example, when we go hunting together, we all share what we caught right?"

"True," they replied.

"In your case," said Brave. "Crown found the cave. Leo led you into the cave and Rose found the sparkling gem .You all had an adventure together so all of you should share the gem that you found."

"But how can we share the gem?" asked Crown.

"There are many ways to share with each other," said Brave.

"You can decide that each one will get to play with the gem for one day , or you can play with it together when all three of you meet, or you might try to find more gems and replace them between you and play with all of them. You will decide how to share, as long as you will share. Because that's what best friends do."

"Great idea," said Crown. "Let's play with the gem together. Okay?"

"Agreed," said Rose and Leo.

"But one moment," said Crown. "There is another problem. We tried to move the gem, but we couldn't move it."

"I know," laughed Brave. "I didn't tell you this before, but you found the sharing gem. This magical gem was lost in the cave many years ago. Only those who are willing to share it with others will be able to move it."

"So what should we do?," asked Leo.

"Go back to the cave," said Brave. "And lift the gem together. Then you will be able to share it and play with it."

Leo, Rose and Crown hurried back to the cave.

They held the gem together and succeeded to move it quickly from its stone shelf.

"Once we agreed to share," said Leo. "Everything became easy."

"Now we all can enjoy more," said Rose.

"Let's go outside and play with the magic gem," said Crown.

Cheerful and happy all three friends went out of the cave to the valley tossing the magic gem up in the air and laughing out loud.

A Note from the Author

To my dear readers:

Thank you for purchasing "The Sharing Lion"

I really enjoyed writing it and I've already had some great feedback from kids and parents who enjoyed the story and illustrations. I hope you too enjoyed it.

I appreciate that you choose to buy and read my book over some of the others out there. Thank you for putting your confidence in me to help educate and entertain your kids.

If you'd like to read another book of mine , I've included it on the next page for you.

Sincerely yours

Efrat Haddi

More GREAT books by Efrat Haddi

The Caring Knight

Efrat Haddi   Illustrations - Abira Das

The Persistent Owl

Efrat Haddi

Illustrations - Abira Das

The Forgiving Lion

Efrat Haddi

Illustrations - Abira Das

The Time Fairy

Efrat Haddi

Illustrations - Abira Das

THE DRAGON
IN ME

Efrat Haddi   Illustrations - Abira Das

Lily's Shy Parrot

Efrat Haddi

Illustrations - Abira Das

Magic Seeds
of Patience

Efrat Haddi

Illustrations - Abira Das

Magic Seeds
of Patience

Efrat Haddi
Illustrations - Abira Das

Lily's Shy Parrot

Efrat Haddi
Illustrations - Abira Das

THE DRAGON
IN ME

Efrat Haddi   Illustrations - Abira Das

The Time
Fairy

Social Skills for Kids
Collection

Das

Made in the USA
Middletown, DE
28 June 2017